The Metamorphosis

A Play

Adapted by E. Thomalen

Based on a Novella by Franz Kafka

Baker's Plays
7611 Sunset Blvd.
Los Angeles, CA 90042
bakersplays.com

DEDICATION

To Francine L. Trevens who graciously took on the difficult task of being the first to realize this work on stage and assembled, and directed, a very talented cast. She helped me better understand the play. This book is dedicated to her with great appreciation for her effort and her talent.

E. Thomalen

The Metamorphosis—A Play is a dramatic adaptation of Kafka's novella. The story, first published in 1915, is of a man who finds himself transformed one day into an insect. There is a tragicomic dimension to this surreal tale. In E. Thomalen's adaptation Gregor Samsa awakens *into* a dream. In this nightmare he can neither speak nor alter the conduct of those around him who see him as a bug. A musician communicates his emotions. All action takes place in the moment of the dream rather than in real time. Inviting the audience to view the experience as Gregor perceives it, the Stage Manager summons the play. Set in early 20th century Prague and written in verse, this new adaptation captures the surreal humor and pathos of the story. Is there anyone who has not been such an outsider?

Reviewer's comments of the 2003 Off Broadway production at the Jose Quintero Theatre in New York City include: *Off Off Broadway Review*: "highly recommended"; *Hi Drama*: "This adaptation makes one ponder socially significant issues, class struggles, inequities, treatment of someone different-i.e., Disabled or dysfunctional and the writing is forthright"; *Town and Village* wrote: "Thomalen has done the theater-going public a great service"; *Talkin Broadway*: "Franz Kafka's *The Metamorphosis* begins as the story's central figure, Gregor Samsa, becomes a giant insect. Stories seldom start in a more over-the-top, theatrical way...a rich subject...how would Gregor be represented? Thomalen's solution is both obvious and effective, having the actor portraying him (Kevin Whittinghill) never utter a single spoken line, with whatever insect-like speech he can muster portrayed by Klezmer-like violin sounds being produced by the Hasidic musician (David Kornhaber) who always accompanies Gregor...Whittinghill gives one of the most convincing performances in the play, his movements stylized, and his overall manner one of the way a cockroach might impersonate a human...".

OFF BROADWAY DEBUT
New York City January 9, 2003

Jose Quintero Theatre
StageRight Productions Inc.

Adapted by: E. Thomalen
Directed by: Francine Trevens

MRS. SAMSA......................................Loretta Guerra Woodruff
MR. SAMSA..Peter J. Coriaty
GRETE SAMSA............................Jessica Greenberg, Alexis Wickwire
GREGOR.......................................Kevin Whittinghill
STAGE MANAGER............................Marcalan Glassberg
OFFICE MANAGER............................David Lamberton
MAID....................................Ozlem Turhal, Joanna Stavros
FIRST BOARDER.................................David Lamberton
SECOND BOARDER.............................Brandon DeSpain
THIRD BOARDER..............................Marcalan Glassberg
CLEANING WOMAN...............Ozlem Turhal, Joanna Stavros
KLEZMER MUSICIAN............................David Kornhaber

Set and Costume Design: T. Silver,
Lighting Design: Sherrian Felix
Publicity: Judd Hollander, Brett Singer
Managing Producer: Maitely Weismann

ACTS

CHARACTERS:

GREGOR SAMSA ....late twenties; a dung beetle
                                             or believes self to be
GRETE SAMSA ....late teens; Gregor's sister
MR. SAMSA ....mid-fifties; Gregor's father
MRS. SAMSA ....early fifties; Gregor's mother
OFFICE MANAGER
FIRST MAID
CLEANING WOMAN
FIRST BOARDER
SECOND BOARDER
THIRD BOARDER
STAGE MANAGER
THE FIDDLER

The play is written in a modified Cinquain verse form. If spoken with
end-stopped lines, it approximates the cadence of middle European
speech in American English even without accents.

ACT I– SCENE 1

(This is a dreamscape scene. The stage is divided into two rooms. Stage left is Gregor's bedroom, stage right a turn of the century parlor with a small round dining table covered with a long, lace cloth and set with dishes for breakfast. At the table are Gregor's *parents,* **MR.** *and* **MRS. SAMSA,** *and his sister* **GRETE.** *There is a grandfather clock in one corner, also two settees and a buffet with drawers. The furniture is all slightly askew. There is a door in the back wall. To the far left of the parlor, downstage, is a passage to the kitchen, upstage left a door to the bedroom of Mr. and Mrs. Samsa. In Gregor's bedroom there is a bed, a desk, a chest of drawers, and beside his bed a hard wooden chair. The wall between the two rooms is suggested rather than real, so* **GREGOR** *can react to what he overhears from the Parlor.*

The play opens with a spotlight on the **STAGE MANAGER** *speaking his lines and only Gregor's room is fully illuminated. The cast freezes in place whenever* **GREGOR** *moves).*

STAGE MANAGER.
>Gregor awoke
>From disturbing dreams.
>Gregor awoke
>From shocking screams,
>In his head,
>Thought he was dead,
>Transformed
>Into an Insect,
>For all to Inspect,
>And Reject!

Left Derelict.
The prospect,
Of what to expect,
From the schemes
In his dreams,
Whether substance or smoke,
Is here performed
For our Gregor,
The Traveler
And Seller,
And you folk!

*(The clock ticks loudly. **GREGOR** tosses in bed under the covers. On the chair beside his bed sits the **FIDDLER** in Hasidic dress who plays Klezmer music, alternatingly wildly rapturous and poignantly sad. Finally, **GREGOR** tosses off the comforter and emerges on his back, wriggling arms and legs on top of his bed. He has a large painted tear under his upstage eye. The audience must be made more aware of the man in the bug, than of the bug in the man. The light in Gregor's room dims and that in the parlor comes up.)*

MR. SAMSA.
The eggs
were a little
over cooked this morning,
and not exactly to my taste,
please tell the maid,
And pass,
please, the coffee.
Grete, please pass the marmalade.

GRETE SAMSA.
Yes, yes
Father, I will.

MRS. SAMSA.

> I shall
> say something to
> the maid about the eggs.
> But don't you think that Gregor works
> too hard?

MR. SAMSA.

> He is
> a good boy, they
> take advantage of him.
> His boss has a very hard heart,
> like flint.
> He gets up at
> Four to catch the train at
> Five o'clock and if a salesman
> is not
> on it by then
> a person from the firm
> reports it to the manager
> and he
> could be finished!

> *(GREGOR turns over onto his hands and knees and holds his head with both hands while the FIDDLER plays "groaning" music.)*

> Traveling salesmen of
> other firms live like Harem girls,
> up at
> ten and having
> breakfast when Gregor
> is writing down his morning sales.
> He has
> told it to me,
> That *very* thing, *himself!*

MRS. SAMSA.

> I wish
> he could leave that
> wretched, oppressive firm.

GRETE SAMSA.

> But, but...
> Mother, have you
> forgotten about my
> grand lessons on the violin?
> How could
> we afford them?

MR. SAMSA

> To say
> nothing of *our*
> loan to his firm. No, I
> am afraid he must continue
> there for
> five or six years,
> there really is nothing
> that can be done about it now.
> Besides,
> it is useful
> training for a young man.
> Yes, and a recommendation
> will not
> be dismissed with
> slight regard, *lightly*, by
> Another firm. Certainly it
> will be
> given great weight.
> He is building up his
> contacts. That is the main idea
> in sales.

*(**GREGOR** nods "yes" and the **FIDDLE** again groans)*

Put *thoughts*
of his leaving
out of your mind. It is
impossible!

MRS. SAMSA.
Of course
you are right, but ...

MR. SAMSA.
"But?" No
'but's' about it!

MRS. SAMSA.
But...but
you see it is
now after six-thirty ...

MR. SAMSA.
Of course
it is after
six-thirty, what of it?

MRS. SAMSA.
Gregor
hasn't left yet...

*(**GREGOR** shakes his head)*

GRETE SAMSA.
Not *left?*

MR. SAMSA.
Not left?
Not left *yet!* You
must be wrong...mistaken.

MRS. SAMSA.
I hear
him leave in the
mornings, usually, and I didn't

hear him
leave *this* morning.

GRETE SAMSA.
Mother,
maybe you just
slept through it. Couldn't that be?

MRS. SAMSA.
That has
never happened
before!

MR. SAMSA.
Of course!
That's it. This is
The first time. I always
sleep through it. When he comes home and
when he
leaves, it is not
As important to me. I know
that he
will be back and
that he will leave again.
That is the way it is. That's all.
Nothing
to make a fuss
about, nothing to lose
sleep for.

MRS. SAMSA.
I am
certain that he
has not left this building
today!

MR. SAMSA.
Well then,
knock on his door

and satisfy yourself
if you are so certain of that.

MRS. SAMSA.
I will.

*(**SHE** goes over to his bedroom door and knocks softly)*

Gregor, it is
a quarter to seven. Didn't
you want to catch the train today?

*(**GREGOR** becomes more agitated on his knees on the
bed, and pantomimes "Yes, yes...Mother, thank you." but
does not speak while the **FIDDLER** plays agitated
strains.)*

MR. SAMSA.   *(Going over to the door and knocking louder)*
Gregor,
Gregor, what is
this that is going on?

GRETE SAMSA.
Gregor?
What's the matter?
Can we get you something?
Is there something we could do, please?

MR. SAMSA.
Gregor!
Gregor could that
be you *still* there, just now?

*(**GREGOR** moves agitatedly back and forth on the bed
and the **FIDDLER** plays music which conveys his
distress.)*

GRETE SAMSA.
>Could that
>Be *our* Gregor,
>not on his way to work,
>Mother?

MR. SAMSA.
>He has
>just a sore throat,
>an occupational
>hazard with no known antidote
>for a
>salesman, of course.
>And if he travels, well...
>Gregor?
>Gregor! Gregor!

MRS. SAMSA.
>He is
>awake, no need
>to speak in such a shrill
>manner to him. The offices
>of the
>firm open at
>seven.

(The clock on the wall strikes 7 A.M.)

MR. SAMSA.
>And when
>the messenger
>reports that Gregor has
>not caught his train punctually...

GRETE SAMSA.
>Then the
>manager will
>come here.

*(**GREGOR** covers his face)*

MR. SAMSA.
> That man
> believes that the
> world is just divided
> into two kinds of people, those
> who are
> well, and those who
> don't *want to work!* The firm's
> health insurance doctor never
> argues
> with him, *always*
> goes along with him. Yes?

*(**GREGOR** nods "yes" and the **FIDDLER** plays very
anguished music)*

> No question! Business, that is all
> they have
> interest in,
> business, yes, and making
> money.

GRETE SAMSA.
> They have
> no regard for
> those who work for them. None!

MRS. SAMSA.
> Gregor
> lately has not
> been doing so well. He
> has told me not to worry; but,
> I know
> he has not been
> able to write orders,

as many as he would like to,
as they
would like him to.
It has been a worry
for him.

(The doorbell rings)

GRETE SAMSA.
It is
someone from the
office.

*(The **MAID** emerges from the kitchen)*

MAID.
Shall I
get the door? Yes?
MR. SAMSA.
Yes, yes
Anna, please do!
MRS. SAMSA.
Gregor
will be in for
grief now.

*(The **OFFICE MANAGER** enters wearing a coat, dressed in a business suit, squeaky patent leather shoes, and carrying a cane. Just as he enters the room, **GREGOR** extends himself head first over the edge of the bed and falls loudly to the floor.)*

OFFICE MANAGER.
Something
fell in there, yes?

GRETE SAMSA. *(Moving close to Gregor's door—whispering)*
Gregor,
the manager
is here.

MR. SAMSA.
Gregor,
the manager
has come! He wants to know
why you didn't catch the early
train, please?
What should we say
to him.
Besides, he wants
to speak with you personally.
So please
open the door.
He will *certainly* be
so kind as to excuse any
likely
disorder of
your room.

OFFICE MANAGER.
Hello,
and Good *morning*
Mr. Samsa.

MRS. SAMSA.
There is
something wrong with
him, believe me, there is
a *something* the matter with him.
How else
would Gregor have
missed a train? That boy has
nothing on his mind but business.
It has

11

almost begun
to rile me that he does
not go out nights. He's been back here
in the
city for eight
days now, but every night
he's been *home*. He sits there 'till late
with us,
at the table,
quiet,
reading the paper or
studying, hard, the timetables.

*(**GREGOR** frantically scurries back and forth not
knowing what to do while the **FIDDLER** again plays
agitated music.)*

It is
a distraction
for him when he makes use
of his fretsaw. He used to be
a good
worker of wood.
Why, truly in the space
of two or three evenings he'd
carve a
small picture frame.
You would be amazed at
how pretty it is, it hangs in
his room.
You will see it,
right away, when Gregor
opens the door. You know I'm glad
that you
have come, sir. Yes!

We would never have got
Gregor to open the door or
come out
just by ourselves;
he's so stubborn! And there
is certainly something wrong with
him, though
he couldn't say so...
this morning...or what it was.

OFFICE MANAGER.

I have
not another
explanation myself.
I hope it is not serious.
But on
the other hand,
I must say we at the
firm are *businessmen*—that may be
either:
fortunate or,
perhaps, unfortunate;
whichever you prefer—very
often
we simply must
overcome any slight
"indisposition" for business
reasons.

MR. SAMSA.

So, can
the manager
come in now, please, Gregor?

(He knocks again on the door. **GREGOR** *pantomimes
"yes" and "no".* **GRETE** *begins to weep. During the*
OFFICE MANAGER*'s speech* **GREGOR** *moves*

*toward the door and tries to stand up and open it,
alternating with listening to the speech.)*

OFFICE MANAGER.
Mister
Samsa, what's the
matter? You barricade
yourself into your room, answer
only,
well... nothing, and
cause your family some
serious, *unnecessary*
worry,
and you neglect
—I mention this only
in passing—your duties to the...
well the...
company in
a really shocking way.
I am speaking here in the name
of your
parents and your
employer and ask you
in all *seriousness!* for a
clear and
immediate
explanation. I am
amazed. *Shocked!* I thought I knew you
to be
a calm, quiet,
reasonable person,
and now you suddenly seem to
begin
strutting about,
even flaunting strange whims!

The head of the firm did suggest
to me
this morning an
explanation for your
tardiness—it concerned the cash
payments
recently, that
were entrusted to you;
—but, well, I practically gave
my word,
pledged my honor,
that this explanation
could *not* be right! But now, seeing
your strange
obstinacy,
incomprehensible,
I am about to lose even
the least
desire to stand
up for you in any
way at all. And your job is not
the most
secure, I need
not add! I intended
to tell you all this in private,
but since
you make me waste
my time here for *nothing,*
I don't see why your parents should
not hear
it too. Of *late*
your performance has been
very unsatisfactory;
I know
it is not the

best season for selling,
we all recognize that; but a
season
for not doing
any business at all,
there is no such thing! No, Mister
Samsa,
a thing like that
Cannot be, *will not be,* condoned
by our good directors.

MRS. SAMSA.

Sir, *please,*
I ask you to
be patient, calm yourself.
Whatever has happened to him,
indeed,
could happen to…
anyone, even you!
I am sure it is just a slight,
very
slight, or maybe
not, "indisposition".
He spoke of a forewarning of
illness
last night. He didn't
look healthy but how could
I tell in the light of a lamp?
He should
have reported
it immediately
to the office. But one always
thinks: 'I
can get over
a sickness without my
staying home.' I am sure that there

is *no*
basis for the
head of the firms accusation
about
the cash payments
and I saw him working
on orders last night to send in.
These few
extra hours
of rest have done him some
good, I'm sure of it, and he will
be on
the road with the
eight o'clock train. Don't let
us keep you Sir, and please give our
respects
to the head of
the firm!

OFFICE MANAGER.
I should
like to hear it
from Mister Samsa's lips.

*(The **FIDDLER** plays wildly while **GREGOR** buries his head.)*

Did you
discern a word?
Is he not attempting
to make fools of us here, perhaps?

MRS. SAMSA.
My God,
maybe he is
seriously ill and
we are torturing him. Grete.

Grete!
GRETE SAMSA.
Mother?

(The violin screeches)

MRS. SAMSA.
Go to
the doctor's *now*,
immediately! For
Gregor is sick. Hurry, get the
doctor.
Did you just *hear*
Gregor?
OFFICE MANAGER.
That was
the sound of an
animal…yes?
MR. SAMSA.
Anna!

(Clapping his hands)

Anna! Get a
locksmith quickly! Run! Run!

*(The **GIRLS** run out leaving the door open, then speaking
to the **OFFICE MANAGER**)*

You see, sir, we are *certainly*
doing
all that *we* can
to get help for him here!

*(**GREGOR** now standing upright, tries to open the door, but cannot find a way to do it. He beats silently on it. Finally he reaches into his pocket and finds a hand lever which he places onto the imaginary door.)*

OFFICE MANAGER.
> Listen,
> he turns the
> handle.

*(**GREGOR** continues to dance around, trying to get the door lever to open the door. He presses against the door with his whole weight. Suddenly there is a click as the latch gives way and he slowly pulls the door back towards himself. When it is "opened", seeking to remain upright, he slowly works his way around the door into view but then falls onto his hands and knees before the **OFFICE MANAGER**.)*

> Oh my...

*(The **OFFICE MANAGER** puts his hand over his mouth and backs slowly away, toward the front door and the outside landing.)*

> I must go now...
> To the office... I shall
> give an exact account of things.

(HE continues to back slowly away.)

MRS. SAMSA.   *(She takes two steps towards **GREGOR** and sinks in the midst of her skirts, her head down.   She turns toward the **OFFICE MANAGER**.)*
Please don't
make things harder
for him than they *already* are.
Stick up
for him...there... please.
Traveling salesmen are not liked

(agitated music)

at the office,
I know.
But still a man,
any man, might find for
a time that he was unable
to work,
but that's just the
right time to remember
his past accomplishments and to
keep in
mind that later,
when the obstacle has
been removed, he's bound to work the
harder
and even more
effectively, for sure.
You sir, have a better viewpoint,
just, sir,
between us two,
than the
head of the firm,
himself, who as an
owner

can far, *far* too
easily let his own
judgment be swayed against someone
working
for him there. You,
I know, are aware that
the traveling salesman who is
out of
the office for
practically the whole
year around, can *too* easily
become
the victim of
gossip, coincidences, and
even
unfounded and
unfair accusations!
Against which he is *completely*
helpless!
Unable to
defend himself! Sir, do
not go away without a word
from you
to reassure
me that you think I could
be, *at least partly*, correct. *Please*!

(**GREGOR** *begins to crawl in the direction of the* **MANAGER**, *making supplicating gestures.*)

OFFICE MANAGER.
Goodbye.

(Quickly turns and leaves)

MRS. SAMSA. *(Leaning forward she stares in **GREGOR**'s direction not seeing him. Then suddenly focusing on him.)*

Help! Help!
for God's sake help!

*(With her head tilted forward, **SHE** leaps backward and bumps the table with the breakfast dishes on them and knocks some of the dishes over, including the coffee pot which drips coffee on the floor. **GREGOR** snaps his jaws at the sight of the spilling coffee. Seeing this **MRS. SAMSA** flees to **MR. SAMSA** and falls into his arms.)*

OFFICE MANAGER.
Aagh Aagh

*(His voice is heard reverberating down the whole staircase. **MRS. SAMSA** releases herself from **MR. SAMSA** and goes over to a window to open it and bring in some fresh air. **MR. SAMSA** grabs the manager's cane that he left in his hasty departure and takes a folded newspaper from the table, and rolling it up, he steps in front of **GREGOR**, holding both objects out and stamps his foot forcing **GREGOR** backwards.)*

MR. SAMSA.
Back! Back!

*(**GREGOR** pantomimes "No! No!" He tries to back up but has difficulty, then slowly turns around, throwing apprehensive glances at his father. In order to negotiate himself through the doorway it is necessary for **GREGOR** to raise one side of his body, but in spite of that he still gets stuck. His **FATHER** comes up and with his foot, gives*

*him a hard shove into the room, injuring **GREGOR** on the doorjamb. After **GREGOR**, bleeding, is in his room, **MR. SAMSA** slams the door behind him and all is quiet.)*

ACT II–SCENE 1

*(The scene opens with **GREGOR** cowering under his bed, a small bowl of milk is on the floor inside the door. The **FIDDLER**, still seated next to **GREGOR**'s bed, plays a very melancholy tune. At the table are **MR.** and **MRS. SAMSA** and **GRETE** for the mid day meal. The **MAID** enters and serves the food, she turns suddenly to **MRS. SAMSA**.)*

MAID.

 Mistress
 Samsa please, I
 beg you!

MRS. SAMSA.

 What?...Why
 Anna, my dear...

 *(**GREGOR** stirs himself, listening)*

MAID.

 Please! Please!
 You have been so good
 to me, both of you, all of you...

23

MR. SAMSA.

Yes, Yes!
What *is* it please
dear girl?

MAID.

I beg
you to release
me... *now*!

MRS. SAMSA.

A strange
request! Why you
told me only the other day
how pleased
you were to work
for us.

MAID.

I did,
its just...it seems...
Well things have changed. That's it
you see!

MRS. SAMSA.

What will
you do? Have you
secured another position?

MAID.

No. But..
I shall find one...
just as soon as I can.

MRS. SAMSA.

Really?
If you *must* leave
you must,
but you may continue
with us as long as you like or...
until

you can find a
situation to your
liking.

MAID.

No!

MRS. SAMSA.

No?

MAID.

Please, I
beg you, dismiss
me ...now, right away. Please!

(SHE falls to her knees, her hands pressed together)

MRS. SAMSA.

Dear girl,
please, have something
to eat before you go.

MAID.

No! Please...

MRS. SAMSA.

Well, if
it is your wish
I give you your release,
as of this moment. You are free
to leave!

MAID.

Mistress
thank you, thank you!
And you, also, Mister
Samsa, and Miss Samsa, thank you.
I do
not know how I
can show my gratitude enough.
I will

not *breathe* a word
of anything outside
of this house. You can *count* on me.
Not *one*
single word, I
promise! What others don't
know, they shall not find out from *me*.
Not a
syllable to
a soul.
You can trust me.
You will have no cause to
regret giving me my release.
Banish
any doubt... I
am in your debt, you have
done me a great *favor*, a *great*
favor!
You can rely
on me to do my part.
Thank you.

(*Kisses* **MRS. SAMSA**'s *hand*)

I am
all packed, good bye.

(*SHE goes into the kitchen, picks up a bag and leaves*)

MRS. SAMSA.
What are
we to do now?
GRETE SAMSA.
We must
try to be brave.

MRS. SAMSA.
>Do you
>think that we will
>be able to find *anyone*
>who would ...
>work for us ... now?

>*(**GREGOR** drops his head down, sadly.)*

MR. SAMSA.
>She was
>simply much too
>sensitive, fastidious; and
>*very*
>emotional.
>Her temperament was
>not suitable. I knew it from
>the start.
>I humored her, but
>I knew it *all along*.
>I knew it would come to this, yes...
>over
>one thing or else
>another. Yes, of course
>we will find someone, someone who
>will not
>be like Anna
>so... particular. Now,
>please, do not let this good food go
>to waste.
>Grete, you have
>hardly eaten a bite!

GRETE SAMSA.
>Thank you,
>Father, but I
>have had enough today.

MRS. SAMSA. *(to MR. SAMSA)*
>You have
>scarcely touched anything.

MR. SAMSA.
>I have
>no appetite.

GRETE SAMSA.
>Father,
>wouldn't you like
>a beer
>here with your meal?

MRS. SAMSA.
>Yes, yes
>Grete, you are
>right, a beer is just the
>thing to encourage your Father's
>hunger.
>We must keep up
>our strength.

GRETE SAMSA.
>Father,
>please say 'yes', that
>you will have a beer. You
>have always liked that in the past.
>I will
>gladly go out
>and bring a bottle home.
>It would only take a minute.
>If you
>don't want me to
>then I'll ask the janitor's wife.

She is
always pleased to
run a little errand for us.

MR. SAMSA.

No. No!
Thank you but no.

MRS. SAMSA.

What will
become of us?

GRETE SAMSA.

How shall
we all manage?

MR. SAMSA.

I have
been thinking hard
about that, very hard.

MRS. SAMSA.

Gregor
is certainly
unable to go back
to the firm in his present state.

GRETE SAMSA.

No. He
must not!

MRS. SAMSA.

This is
all so... sudden,
so...well...*unexpected!*

GRETE SAMSA.

Maybe
Gregor will be
like this for the rest of
his life.

MRS. SAMSA.

> My poor
> dear boy. I am
> certain that it is just
> temporary. We must try to
> survive
> until he is
> restored.
> Father will have a
> plan. Yes?

GRETE SAMSA.

> Without
> the commissions
> that Gregor made off his
> work as a salesman we will have
> nothing
> more to live on.

MR. SAMSA.

> Let me
> get out my strong
> lock box.

*(Goes over to the buffet and opens a cabinet in it and pulls out a small box, **GREGOR** is quite interested)*

> This has
> all our records
> in it.

MRS. SAMSA.

> What good
> are old records
> right now?

MR. SAMSA.

> What good
> indeed? Now let

me see ...

*(Pulls out several keys and unlocks two different locks on
the box. When the box is open HE pulls out several small
note books)*

Ah, here it is

(HE removes a thick sheaf of bills).

MRS. SAMSA.
That is
wonderful, yes,
wonderful! We are not
so poor!

(SHE clasps her hands together)

MR. SAMSA.
When my
business failed
five years ago I took
some cash out of the company
and put
it away here.
GRETE SAMSA.
Did the
firm know? Gregor's
firm, did they know of it?
MR. SAMSA.
No! Of
course not. They don't
know anything about it! "Rien"!

GRETE SAMSA.
> Gregor,
> did he know of
> it? Anything at all?

MR. SAMSA.
> No. What
> was the point in
> telling him? Besides, he
> never
> asked, his only
> thought was to go to work
> for the firm to help us out. Why
> should I
> burden him about this?

GRETE SAMSA.
> Poor boy,
> he should have been
> informed. He might have felt
> easier that he could have left
> the firm
> before all this.

MR. SAMSA.
> Why should
> he want to quit?
> Besides, if this money
> had gone to reduce the debt to
> that firm
> we would not have
> it now.

MRS. SAMSA.
> Yes, your
> Father is right!

GRETE SAMSA.
>Is that
>just the money
>from the failed business?

MR. SAMSA.
>Oh no.

MRS. SAMSA.   *(Alarmed)*
>Where else
>is it from then?

MR. SAMSA.
>Gregor
>gave me his check
>to pay the household bills
>and the loan to the firm, I paid
>all of
>them, on time and
>to the penny, each month.
>If there was something left over,
>I put
>it right in *here.*

>(**GREGOR** *covers his face.*)

GRETE SAMSA.
>You did
>not pay off the
>debt with it as he thought?

MR. SAMSA.
>How could
>I be sure that
>something like this *wouldn't* happen?

MRS. SAMSA.
>Don't ask
>such accusing
>questions! Gregor would have

been pleased
at his Father's
foresight!

Even
One ought to, *I*
think, congratulate him.
Mister Samsa, you are a great
decent,
conscientious
human being, not to
mention humble for speaking to
no one
else about it.
You did not keep quiet
because it was shameful or in
any
way reprehensible.
It was
only concern
for others and...his prudence
that kept
our good Father silent,
and so
financially ...
Well off.
MR. SAMSA.
Thank you,
my dear.

GRETE SAMSA.
>It is
>wonderful that
>you salvaged the money, Father.

MR. SAMSA.
>It is
>a large amount
>of money, nevertheless, it
>is not
>*so* large that we
>can in any way manage off
>of just
>the interest
>alone. Indeed, the principal
>itself
>will only last
>us about a year, or
>at most two, if we must use it
>to meet
>all our current
>needs. Therefore, we shall have
>to make
>sacrifices.

MRS. SAMSA.
>I don't
>know what we could
>do without, why *everything*
>is *essential.*

GRETE SAMSA.
>I shall
>give up my violin
>lessons
>and help Mother.

MR. SAMSA.

> Good! I
> may be able
> to help, also.

GRETE SAMSA.

> Father,
> you have helped by
> saving the money. You
> must not try to go back to work.
> Your heart
> and lungs would not
> permit
> it, I do not
> believe.

MRS. SAMSA.

> Grete
> is doubtless right!

MR. SAMSA.

> We shall
> see. Maybe if
> it is the ideal job.
> Who knows?

MRS. SAMSA.

> I am
> sorry but that
> *cannot* be permitted!

MR. SAMSA.

> We must
> do what we must
> do. Now,
> that is all I
> want to hear about it.

MRS. SAMSA.

> I will
> clear the table.

GRETE SAMSA.

> Oh no,
> Mother. It has
> already been an exhausting
> morning
> for you…and Father too.
> Why don't
> you both go now
> to your room and rest and
> I will clear it.

MRS. SAMSA.

> Oh, I
> can not allow
> you to
> do that. It is
> my work.

GRETE SAMSA.

> I don't
> mind, I am not
> tired and I need to
> keep busy. Please *believe* me, you
> would be
> doing me a
> favor.

MRS. SAMSA.

> Well then,
> if you are *sure*
> it would not be too much
> trouble.
> Thank you my dear,
> I will accept your suggestion.

MR. SAMSA.

> Yes, I
> could use a nap

right now.
Until later...
GRETE SAMSA.
Rest well.

*(**MR.** and **MRS. SAMSA** rise from the table and exit
into their bedroom. **GREGOR** scuttles back under his
bed.)*

I had to get
them to leave so that I
could look in on Gregor. I hope
he has
been able to
eat the bread and milk that
I left for him, he used to be
so fond
of it before.

*(SHE walks to Gregor's room. **GREGOR** peers out
from under his bedding. Grete entering cautiously, looks
around.)*

He could
not just have flown
away, he must be here,
there, or... somewhere.

*(SHE catches sight of her brother beneath the bed and
jumps back slamming the door closed.)*

Good Lord
protect me, please!

That's sad
he's not eaten
any of it. Maybe
he is not hungry. But he has
not had
anything to
eat since dinner yesterday and
I am
sure that even
in his present condition he
cannot
go for *very*
long without eating or a meal.
Maybe
what I brought him
no longer appeals to him ... in
this state.
That must be it.
I will need to learn what
to bring my dear brother so long
as he
is in his... well...
present form. But how will
I find that out? I know! I shall
bring him
different sorts
of food
and see which ones
he chooses for himself.

Gregor,
here are some things
from last night's meal, here are
some old bones, some vegetables
here are
some fresh raisins
and almonds, here is a
slice of plain bread and here one with
butter.
Here is a piece
of old cheese, you thought it
was spoiled
two days ago.

I shall
leave, he will be
too embarrassed in his
current likeness to eat in front
of me.
He has always
had a sense of delicacy.

*pleasurable anticipation. He goes over to the paper and after looking it over finds the cheese, and drags it away from the rest, devours it first with great pleasure. The **MUSICIAN** again plays ecstatically)*

ACT II–SCENE 2

*(It is two months later. **MRS. SAMSA** and **GRETE** are seated at the table in the parlor. There is a bowl of apples on the table. **GREGOR** and the musician share the chair in Gregor's room. The **FIDDLER** plays a melancholy tune and **GREGOR** stares out the window, his back to the parlor.)*

GRETE SAMSA.
> Can it
> be the same man?

MRS. SAMSA.
> I would
> never have believed it.

GRETE SAMSA.
> It is
> a miracle,
> he used to be, well, so
> sluggish, he put on so much weight.

MRS. SAMSA.
> Why, it
> is like the past
> five years were suddenly
> erased.

I have always
said that his business
failure
aged him ten years,
no... twenty at the least!

GRETE SAMSA.
He used
to be in bed
when Gregor left for business
in the
morning, and when
he returned in the evening
he would
still be sitting
in his bathrobe. He could
not rise to greet Gregor, but would
only
raise his arms
to show his pleasure at
seeing
Gregor once more.

MRS. SAMSA.
In the
park on Sundays
he could not keep up. Even you
and I,
who, it surely
must be said, are not the fastest
walkers,
would have to slow
down for
Father.

GRETE SAMSA.
He would
shuffle along

in his old over coat,
even in June, so carefully
planting
his cane with each
new step of his progress.
MRS. SAMSA.
And if
he had something
to say he would call us
to stop
and assemble
around him and we would
have to wait five minutes before
he caught
his breath and was
composed enough to utter it.
GRETE SAMSA.
Father
has become a
different person since
Gregor has undergone his... change.

(Glancing at the clock on the wall)

So, it
is time to clean
his room.
MRS. SAMSA.
You will
tell me how you
find him?
GRETE SAMSA.
Yes, yes.
What ever you
want to know about him.

*(The **FIDDLER** begins to play again. **GRETE** goes to the door and slips into the room. She is startled to see **GREGOR** beside the musician in the chair. SHE jumps back, slams the door, and leans against the door with her eyes closed.)*

MRS. SAMSA.
Why... what
is it, Grete?

GRETE SAMSA.
Nothing!

*(**GREGOR** leaves the chair and scuttles under the bed.)*

MRS. SAMSA.
Is he
alright? Did he
bite you?

GRETE SAMSA.
It is
just that he is ...
in full view, on his chair.
I cannot stand to look at him
or be
in his bedroom
without his being *partly* screened.

MRS. SAMSA.
Perhaps
you should not go
in at this time, you could
do it some other time. I would
surely
not accuse you
of being a hypochondriac.

GRETE SAMSA.

> No, no
> it is my clear
> duty, the least I can
> do for my poor brother. I will
> not be
> sidetracked. I have
> just surprised him, that's all.

> *(SHE turns around and again opens the door, cautiously.
> Seeing the room empty she rushes across it, opens the
> window, breathing deeply several times in front of it. She
> then picks up a broom and a pail left in the room, sweeps
> up the leavings from the last meal and any dirt in the room.
> She puts a lid on the pail and rushes out of the room to the
> kitchen and after emptying it brings the pail and the lid
> back into the room and leaves them beside the broom. She
> then retreats, closes the door without a backward glance.)*

MRS. SAMSA.

> How did
> the room look, dear,
> tell me?

GRETE SAMSA.

> Gregor
> was well behaved.
> He did not come out while
> I was in the room. But he has
> refused
> his food again.

MRS. SAMSA.

> Has he
> shown any, the
> *least,* improvement...whatsoever?

GRETE SAMSA.

> There is
> no change I'm sad
> to say.

MRS. SAMSA.

> Let me
> go to Gregor,
> he is my unfortunate boy.

(SHE rises)

GRETE SAMSA.

> Mother,
> you must not go,
> it would upset you in there.

(SHE rises.)

MRS. SAMSA.

> I must!
> Don't you see? I
> must go to him, my *child*...

(SHE moves toward the door.)

GRETE SAMSA.

> Mother,
> you could not take
> it. Please!

(SHE takes her mother by the shoulders and gently steers her back to her chair.)

MRS. SAMSA.
>I just
>wanted to be
>of help to him, put him
>at ease.

GRETE SAMSA.
>There isn't
>anything that
>you can do for him now.

MRS. SAMSA.
>There must
>be something. Is
>he quite comfortable?

GRETE SAMSA.
>He has
>all that useless
>furniture still in there.
>I believe it is confining
>for him.
>Maybe we could
>move some of it out so
>that he has more freedom to move
>about.
>You could help me
>with it.

MRS. SAMSA.
>Then I
>could go into
>his room!

GRETE SAMSA.
>Yes and
>help me!

MRS. SAMSA. *(Claps her hands and is excited)*
>Yes. Yes.

GRETE SAMSA.
I will
see if all is
in order and if Gregor is
hidden
out of the way.

*(SHE enters the room and seeing that **GREGOR** is well
hidden turns around to her mother.)*

Come on.
You can't see him.

*(When her **MOTHER** enters the room)*

Let's take out the chest of drawers
first…he
does not need it
any longer.

MRS. SAMSA.
The chest?

GRETE SAMSA.
Yes! I
will get behind
it and try to push it,
you work
it from the front.

*(THEY begin to move the chest away from the wall with
many grunts and groans)*

MRS. SAMSA.
> It is
> very heavy,
> maybe we should wait for
> Father.

GRETE SAMSA.
> We can
> do it, we are
> not so helpless as that.

MRS. SAMSA.
> Don't strain
> yourself, my dear.

GRETE SAMSA.
> I'm not!

MRS. SAMSA.
> I am
> worried that you
> will over exert yourself here.

GRETE SAMSA.
> I don't
> feel it at all.

MRS. SAMSA.
> We won't
> be able to
> do it and if we leave
> it in the middle of the room,
> Gregor
> perhaps will be
> barricaded in. No!
> It is better to leave it where
> it was.

GRETE SAMSA.
> We can
> get it all the

way out of the room with
just a little more effort now.

MRS. SAMSA. *(Whispering and looking around)*
I am
not sure that we
are truly doing Gregor a
favor
by removing
his furniture. It is
heart breaking to see the bare walls
and *why*
shouldn't Gregor
feel the same way, since he
has been used to this furniture
so long
and will likely
feel abandoned in his
empty room. He has had this chest
since he
was a little
boy and he used to do
his homework on that desk. And won't
it look
as if by our
removing these objects
we are showing him that we have
given
up all hope of
his getting better, and
are leaving him to his sad fate
without
any further
consideration? I
think the best idea would be to
try to

keep the room as
it was before, so that
when Gregor comes back to us once
again
he will find things
unchanged and can forget
all the more easily what has
happened
in the meantime.

GRETE SAMSA.
I am
the one who comes
into his room every day
to leave
food and to clean.
I believe that I know
better what Gregor wants than you.
I was
just going to
remove the desk and the
chest of drawers, but I think now
we should
take out all of
his furniture, *everything!*
Even
his bed! Gregor
needs plenty of room to
crawl around in, it is all that
is left
for him to do.

MRS. SAMSA.
Grete,
no one will come
in here but you if it
is just bare walls, and Gregor as

he is...
in his troubled
condition...this room will
be a cave...and he must then
forget
his human past
as a dream, or nothing.

GRETE SAMSA.
I have
to disagree
with you, Mother, I know
what is best for him. Now keep on
pulling
while I push. There
is nothing further to
discuss on this
matter.

(THEY manage to get the chest of drawers out of the room. When they are out of the room **GREGOR** *looks out from under the bed, displeased, but ducks his head back under when his mother reenters while his sister is still rocking the chest back and forth outside of the room. His* **MOTHER** *stops, stands still, having caught the movement of the sheet out of the corner of her eye, and goes back to* **GRETE.** **GREGOR** *comes out from under the bed, worried, changing directions several times, not knowing what to salvage first. He climbs up on the chair and clings to his framed picture so no one could remove it. The WOMEN reenter with Grete's arm around her mother.)*

So, what
shall we take now?

*(SHE looks around and her eyes meet **GREGOR'S** who is on the chair clinging to the picture. She struggles for self-control. To her mother:)*

We had
better go back
into the parlor for
a minute. Come!

MRS. SAMSA.   *(Becoming very anxious and looking around, she sees **GREGOR** on the chair and cries out)*
Oh God!
Oh God help me!

(SHE falls with outstretched arms across Gregor's bed)

GRETE SAMSA.
You, there
Gregor..!

*(SHE glares at **GREGOR** and raises her fist. Then she runs into the next room to get some spirits to revive her mother from one of the cabinets in the buffet. **GREGOR**, wanting to help, gets down from the chair and follows his sister into the parlor. **GREGOR'S** presence startles **GRETE** and she drops a bottle. Grete then grabs an armful of bottles and runs into Gregor's room, slamming the door behind her with her foot. While Grete ministers to her mother, **GREGOR** crawls agitatedly over everything in the parlor while the **FIDDLER** plays sort of "drunken" music. After a short time the doorbell rings and **GRETE** leaves her mother to answer it. It is **MR. SAMSA** and **GRETE** falls against his chest. He is dressed now in a tight fitting sky-blue uniform with gold buttons and braid*

*on his coat, a doorman at an expensive hotel! He has a
cap of the same color, having a gold monogram on the front
of it.)*

MR. SAMSA.
>Grete
>what has happened?

GRETE SAMSA.
>Mother
>fainted, but she
>is better now. Gregor
>has broken out.

MR. SAMSA.
>I knew
>it would happen.
>I kept telling you but
>you women don't want to listen.

GRETE SAMSA.   *(Pushing off from her father)*
>I am
>going back to
>help her.

*(SHE reenters Gregor's room and slams the door shut
again. She proceeds to partly undress her mother so that
her mother can breathe more freely. **GREGOR** backs
himself up against the closed door to his room, indicating
his wish to go back inside and hide once again.)*

MR. SAMSA.
>Aha!

*(**MR. SAMSA** throwing his hat across the room onto the
settee, puts his hands into his pockets and starts towards
GREGOR with an angry look in his eye and lifting his
feet unusually high off the floor. **GREGOR** leaves his post*

in front of the door and runs ahead of his father.
GREGOR *stops when his father does and darts away
when his father makes even the slightest movement. He
finds it difficult to stay ahead of his father as* THEY *circle
the table for a second time. Then, suddenly, his*
FATHER *picks up an apple from the bowl on the table
and throws it at* ***GREGOR*** *and, pleased with himself,*
HE *bombards* ***GREGOR*** *with apples, hitting him
several times. As* ***GREGOR*** *starts to collapse under the
cannonade, the door opens to Gregor's room and* ***MRS.***
SAMSA *comes out with* ***GRETE*** *following her.)*

GRETE SAMSA.
Father!
Please! Don't!

MRS. SAMSA. *(to* ***MR. SAMSA****)*
Please, please!
Don't hurt my poor
changed boy!

(SHE crosses the room to ***MR. SAMSA****, her loosened
skirt and petticoats falling away and grabs* ***MR. SAMSA***
*in a passionate embrace, a complete union, begging for
Gregor's life.)*

I beg you to
spare him please! Don't kill him!

*(****GREGOR*** *slowly makes his retreat into his room
through the open door, but his eyes are fixed backwards on
his parent's erotic display.)*

ACT III–SCENE 1

(It is another month later, **GREGOR** *is in his room near the door which is slightly ajar. The furniture in his room has been restored. The rest of the family are in the parlor around the table.* **MR. SAMSA,** *in his uniform, is asleep in his chair.* **MRS. SAMSA** *sews lingerie which lies on the floor about her, and* **GRETE** *is learning shorthand and French, her books are piled on the table.)*

GRETE SAMSA.   *(loudly)*
Bonjour.
*Comment allez
vous? Bien, et vous?*

MRS. SAMSA.
Shh, you
will wake up your
Father.

GRETE SAMSA.
Wait a
minute. Here it
is: *'Pardonnez moi, s'il
vous plait.'*

MRS. SAMSA.
Why are
you learning French?

GRETE SAMSA.
I am
learning French *and*
shorthand.
I don't want to
be a salesgirl *all* of
my life.

MRS. SAMSA.
>You are
>right. You are... right.

MR. SAMSA. *(Awakening)*
>What is
>it? What is it?

MRS. SAMSA.
>Never
>mind. It's nothing
>that concerns you, Mister Samsa.

MR. SAMSA. *(Looking at his wife's work)*
>Look how
>long you have been
>sewing...
>again today.

>*(HE falls back to sleep and the two WOMEN smile
>wearily.)*

MRS. SAMSA.
>He has
>no idea he's
>been sleeping when he wakes.

GRETE SAMSA.
>Almost
>every night
>he replays this sad scene anew.

MRS. SAMSA.
>He works
>hard and is so
>tired
>each evening.

GRETE SAMSA.
>Father
>is right, Mother.

You put in too many
hours
sewing for that
lingerie store.

MRS. SAMSA.
We need
all the money.
What can I do? Our expenses
are still
so high. Why the
cleaning woman that we
have now costs less than a maid's bill,
but we
cannot manage
without *someone* at all,
especially now that we are
all out working.

GRETE SAMSA.
If we
could only bring
in more
money.

MRS. SAMSA.
Selling
the jewelry
helped for awhile, but now...

GRETE SAMSA.
There is
hardly any
of it left. If we could
just get rid of this apartment
and get
a smaller one,
a less *expensive* one.

(*GREGOR* looks alarmed.)

MRS. SAMSA.
> How could
> we even *think*
> of it ?

GRETE SAMSA.
> It is
> *Gregor* that makes
> it all impossible.

(*GREGOR* hangs his head. The **FIDDLER** plays an
elegiac tune.)

MRS. SAMSA.
> How could
> we move him? And
> who would let rooms to us?

GRETE SAMSA.
> Is there
> anyone who
> ever had to put up
> with such a great and heavy grief?

(*GREGOR*'s tear is very visible.)

MRS. SAMSA.
> A thing
> like this never
> has happened to any of our
> friends, nor
> some relative.
>
> But who would talk about
> it? It is a *great* misfortune.

Grete Samsa.
It must
somehow be a
punishment for God knows...

(Shrugs)

Mrs. Samsa.
Would He
do that for *no*
reason?
Grete Samsa.
It is
all so hopeless.

*(**GREGOR** hangs his head.)*

Mrs. Samsa.
We must
not let Gregor
think we believe that's true.
Grete Samsa.
I am
all worn out from
running back and forth so,
behind the sales counters for the
shoppers
at work that I
don't have the strength to look
after him as well any more.
He will
just have to take
whatever I put out
for him.

*(**GREGOR** scowls.)*

I clean his room
as well as I can now.

*(**GREGOR** indicates his displeasure)*

I can
no longer be
bothered with special treats.
He has been too fussy lately,
even
refusing his
supper. But he will just
have to learn to accept these things.

MRS. SAMSA.
You do
the best you can,
you certainly can't be faulted.

GRETE SAMSA.
What are
we now to do?

MRS. SAMSA.
I have
thought that maybe
we could take in a few
boarders.

*(**GREGOR** is alarmed.)*

GRETE SAMSA.
Where would
we put them, not
in Gregor's room, surely!

MRS. SAMSA.

> Oh No!
> We could give them
> our room, your Father's and
> mine. We will move to the back of
> the flat
> closer to you.

*(**GREGOR** is relieved.)*

GRETE SAMSA.

> It would
> mean more money.
> I could help you take care
> of them.

MRS. SAMSA.

> Yes, it
> might make things a
> little easier, though
> we have never done anything
> like it
> before.

(The clock strikes ten)

> It is
> time to wake your
> Father and put him to
> bed, this room is no place to sleep
> and he
> must have his rest,
> he is needed there by
> six o'clock tomorrow morning.
> Wake up

dear, wake up, please.
It's time to go to bed.

MR. SAMSA.

What? What?
No, I want to
stay here just a little longer.

MRS. SAMSA.

No, no.
It's time to go
to bed,
come on, Mister Samsa.

MR. SAMSA.

No! No!

(Closes his eyes and shakes his head)

MRS. SAMSA.

It is
written: "The sleep
of the laboring man
is sweet."
Come to bed now,
yes, yes
you deserve it.

MR. SAMSA.   *(Continues to shake his head)*

MRS. SAMSA.

If you
come to bed now
I will make it pleasing for you.

*(**MR. SAMSA** continues to shake his head, his WIFE
now standing over him whispers in his ear and HE smiles
but continues to close his eyes and shake his head.)*

GRETE SAMSA.   *(Gets up and stands next to her mother)*
I will
help you, Mother.
Come on,
Father.

(No response)

We will have to
carry him as usual.

*(The WOMEN lift him up under his arms and only then
does HE open his eyes. THEY walk him back towards
his bedroom door.)*

MR. SAMSA.
Ahh what
a *life*.

(Shaking his head)

So *this* is the
peace of my elder years.

*(At the door HE shrugs the women off and proceeds
independently)*

ACT III SCENE 2

*(Yet another month has passed. Gregor's room is now also used for storage, there is a rolled up rug in it, an extra chair and vanity table, the garbage and ash cans and a spare waste basket. There is considerable dirt and dust on the floor. **MRS. SAMSA** and **GRETE** are off stage in the kitchen preparing the evening meal and a **CLEANING WOMAN** with bony limbs and white hair carries an old standing lamp across the parlor to the door to Gregor's room. She puts in inside and seeing **GREGOR**, she speaks.)*

CLEANING WOMAN.
    Come here
    a minute you
    old dung beetle. Look at
    that old dung beetle. Ha Ha Ha!
    Aren't you
    an ugly one,
    a great big *ugly* one.
    I could squash you with my foot in
    no time
    and put you out
    with the trash. Oh am I
    disturbing you? So what does it
    matter
    if this old head
    bothers a *dung* beetle?
    I am not afraid of you. Do
    these things
    get in your way?
    Well, I am *so* sorry.
    You are lucky you have a place

that is
dry and warm, the
rest of it shouldn't cause worry
to an
old dung beetle.
Oh, he doesn't like my
teasing him, eh?

*(**GREGOR** starts to move, slowly and decrepitly toward
the **CLEANING WOMAN**, intending to frighten her.
She picks up a chair and holds it over her head, baring her
teeth at the same time. **GREGOR** stops and timidly
turns around and goes back to his corner)*

So, is
that all there is?

*(SHE puts her chair down and leaves the room, the door
remaining slightly ajar)*

Mistress
Samsa, I'm *finished.*
I'm leaving now. I'll be
here early tomorrow. Good bye.

*(SHE opens the front door to the apartment and yells
back)*

Oh, you
should be informed,
the boarders are coming upstairs.

MRS. SAMSA.
Yes, good.
Very good. Yes.
So until tomorrow ...

*(The **CLEANING WOMAN** leaves and the three*
***BOARDERS** enter, one is tall and the leader, the other*
two are short. They take their coats off and leave them on a
coat stand along with their canes. The taller one goes to the
kitchen door.)

FIRST BOARDER.
> *Madame,*
> I do not mind
> telling you myself that
> we are here and we are hungry.
> Is the
> dinner ready
> for the three of us yet?

MRS. SAMSA.
> Yes, yes
> gentlemen, be
> seated at the table
> if you please, and I will have your
> dinner
> for you in just
> a minute, in no time at all!

MR. SAMSA.   *(Emerges from the kitchen)*
> My wife
> has the dinner
> prepared. Just have a seat
> at the table. Let me help you.

(HE holds the chair for each man and opens the napkin
for him. THEY each nod in acknowledgment. When they
*are all seated, **MRS. SAMSA** and **GRETE** emerge with*
the steaming platters of food. The taller man cuts into the
meat while the other two watch, he indicates his acceptance
and the women emit a sigh of relief and smile.)

Does it,
would you say, meet
with your approval, gentlemen?
If it
doesn't, my wife
will take it back and cook
it a bit more.

FIRST BOARDER.
It is
satisfactory.
Yes.

MRS. SAMSA.
Thank you,
good gentlemen.

*(SHE curtsies. The **BOARDERS** eat in silence while the Samsa's return to the kitchen. After a short interval there is the sweet, sad sound of a violin. The boarders who had taken out their papers and cigars at first ignore it but then become interested and get up and go over to the kitchen door where they stand together. **MR. SAMSA** comes out.)*

MR. SAMSA.
Perhaps
the playing may
bother you gentlemen.
It can be stopped, right now!

FIRST BOARDER.
Oh, on
the contrary,
wouldn't the young lady
like to come in here and play where
it's much
roomier and

more comfortable? She
has such a fine and steady hand.

MR. SAMSA.
Oh, why
certainly! Yes!

*(The **BOARDERS** go back and sit on the settees. **MR.**
SAMSA comes in with the music stand and **MRS.**
SAMSA brings the sheet music, while **GRETE**—followed
by the **FIDDLER** carrying his fiddle and bow— enters.
MR. SAMSA stands in the kitchen doorway with his
hand between two buttons on his uniform coat, **MRS.**
SAMSA takes a seat the boarder has vacated. **GRETE**
pantomimes playing while the **FIDDLER** plays and at
first the **BOARDERS** appear interested, but then they
rise and withdraw to the window and blow cigar smoke at
the ceiling, talking in low tones to one another, clearly
disinterested. **GREGOR**, however, when he first begins to
hear the music, moves slowly to the partly open door. There
he hesitates a moment, then moved by the music, comes
slowly into the parlor. He moves with his head tilted and
close to the floor, hoping to catch his sister's eye.)*

FIRST BOARDER.   *(Amused)*
My host,
so what is this?

*(Pointing to **GREGOR**, **GRETE** stops playing)*

MR. SAMSA.   *(Rushing in front of the boarders with outstretched arms,
herding them back to their room)*
Please, please
Gentlemen, it
is nothing I *assure*

you. Pay it no mind, let me help
you to
my room, I mean ...
your room, it was my room
but now it is your room. You must
be tired,
a good meal will
always make one, well, just
a *little* sleepy. If you will
retire
we will clear the ...
room and will not disturb you this
evening, further.

FIRST BOARDER.

Mister
Samsa, wait! What
is this, what are you trying to
hide here?

MR. SAMSA.

Nothing,
I assure you,
I am not trying to
hide anything from you. Just let
us clear
the table and
put the room in order.

FIRST BOARDER.

We want,
please, an answer!

MR. SAMSA.

There is
nothing to say,
that is just Gregor, he
doesn't

usually
come out into the drawing room.

FIRST BOARDER. *(Stamping his foot and thus stopping* **MR. SAMSA**
from pushing them into their room)
Herewith
I declare that
in view of the revolting state
that does
prevail in this
apartment and this family

(Spitting)

I give
notice as of
today.
Of course, I won't
pay a cent for the time
I have been living here either;
rather,
I shall even
consider taking some
sort of action against you with
claims that—
believe me—will
be easy to substantiate.

SECOND BOARDER.
We, *too,*
give notice as
of now.

(THEY all enter the bedroom slamming the door.
GRETE *puts her face in her hands, shaking her head.*
With the excitement **MRS. SAMSA** *struggles to get her*
breath. After the door to the boarder's room is closed,

MR. SAMSA goes to his chair and collapses in it while
GREGOR lies quietly where he was when the commotion
began.   The FIDDLER slowly, carefully, reenters
Gregor's room.)

GRETE SAMSA.
My dear
parents things can't
go on like this. Maybe

(Pounding the table)

you don't realize it, but I
certainly do.
I won't
pronounce the name
of my brother in front
of this monster, and so all I
can say
is: we have to
try to get rid of it.

(GREGOR hangs his head and the FIDDLER plays
sad music.)

We've done everything that we
can do,
that is at all
humanly possible
to take care of it and to put
up with
it, I don't think
any one can blame us in the
least way.

MR. SAMSA. *(Playing with his uniform cap)*
She is
absolutely
correct.

*(MRS. SAMSA is now coughing behind her hand, a wild
look in her eye, and GRETE goes over to her.)*

GRETE SAMSA. *(To her father)*
We must
try to get rid
of it. It will be the
death of you two, I can see it
coming.
Those who have to
work as hard as we do
already, can't put up with this
constant
torture at home,
also. I cannot stand
it any more.

*(Her tears roll down on her mother who brushes them off
mechanically)*

MR. SAMSA.
Child, tell
me what can we
do then?

(GRETE shrugs, bewildered.)

If he
could just reason
with us ...

*(**GREGOR** holds out his hand begging his Father to
listen to him while the **FIDDLER** plays urgent music)*

If he
could possibly
understand us then maybe we
could come
to some timely
agreement with him. But
the way things are...
GRETE SAMSA.
It has
to *go*. That's the
only answer, Father.

*(**GREGOR** hangs his head)*

You just have to get rid of the
idea
that it's Gregor.
Believing it for so long, that
is our
real misfortune.
But how can it be our
Gregor? If it were really him,
he would
have realized
long ago that it is
not possible for us to live
with such
a creature, and

*(The **FIDDLER** plays very melancholic music)*

he would have gone away

of his own free will. Then we wouldn't
have a
brother, but we
would be able to go
on living and honor his name.
But not
as things are, this
insect persecutes us,
drives the roomers away, even
wants to
occupy the
whole apartment and for
us to sleep out in the gutter.

(Excited)

Look there
Father, he is
starting to move again.

*(SHE leaves her mother and runs behind her father who
stands up. **GREGOR** is only turning around.)*

MR. SAMSA.
He is
going back to
his room.

*(**GREGOR** goes into his room, only looking back sadly at
the doorway. When he is in his room **GRETE** runs over
and slams the door closed, bolting it.)*

GRETE SAMSA.
There! It's
done. *Finally!*

*(The family clears the dinner dishes from the table and exits through the kitchen. The parlor darkens and the cuckoo clock on the wall chimes the hours of the night. At 3 AM. **GREGOR** dies, the **FIDDLER** gets up and moves to the parlor. When the dawn breaks, at 5 AM., the **CLEANING WOMAN** lets herself in through the front door, slamming it closed behind her. She goes first to the kitchen, then to Gregor's room picking up the broom to begin her days work.)*

CLEANING WOMAN.
Wake up
you old cockroach
Wake up! Pretending that you are
asleep
won't do with me.
No, no you can't fool me.
Have I
hurt your feelings,
well, don't expect *me* to
apologize. You can carry
on as
long as you like,
ignoring me, but you
won't hear me say I'm sorry to
an old
foul dung beetle.
But that is *no reason*
to just lie there and not to take
any
notice of this
woman. Have I ever
treated you so badly. Let's see...
are you
ticklish today.

(SHE tries to tickle him with the end of the broom. Then becoming annoyed, she jabs him and finally shoves him without resistance to another part of the room. She whistles, her eyes open wide and she goes quickly to the door.)

Hello
Come, have a look,
it's *croaked!* it's lying there,
just as dead as any doornail.

*(**MR. SAMSA** with a blanket over his shoulders and **MRS. SAMSA** in her night gown appear through the kitchen door and **GRETE** follows, fully dressed, as though she had not slept.)*

MR. SAMSA.
Deceased?
CLEANING WOMAN.
I'll say!

(SHE goes back and pushes Gregor's body again with the broom.)

MR. SAMSA.
Well, now
we can thank God.

(HE clasps his hands in a silent prayer as the others do also.)

GRETE SAMSA.
Just look
how thin he was.
Of course he didn't eat

anything for such a long time.
The dish
came out again
just the way it went in.

MRS. SAMSA.
Come sit
with us for a
little while, please, Grete.

*(**THE SAMSAS** leave Gregor's room and then exit
through the kitchen door. The **CLEANING WOMAN**
opens the window and begins to clean up the room. The
BOARDERS emerge from their room.)*

FIRST BOARDER.
Where is
breakfast today?
SECOND BOARDER.
We want
our morning meal.
CLEANING WOMAN.
Shh. Shh.
Follow me please.

*(SHE takes them into Gregor's room and THEY stare at
the corpse, then emerge from the room.)*

FIRST BOARDER.   *(Loudly)*
Where's the
breakfast?

*(**MR. SAMSA** appears from the kitchen door in his
uniform with **MRS. SAMSA** on one arm and **GRETE**
on the other.)*

MR. SAMSA.

>I find
>your manners *vile*!
>Leave my house immediately!

FIRST BOARDER.

>What do
>you *mean* by that?

SECOND BOARDER.

>Yes, *what?*

MR. SAMSA.

>I mean
>just what I said.

(HE marches the boarders towards the door.)

FIRST BOARDER.

>So... we'll...
>go then.

(THEY take their coats and canes, open the front door and leave. **THE SAMSAS** *go to the door and follow them down the stairs with their eyes. When they are satisfied that they have left the Samsas close the door and come back into the room.)*

MRS. SAMSA.

>It is
>such a lovely
>spring day.

GRETE SAMSA.

>Yes! Yes!
>A wonderful
>fine day!

MR. SAMSA.
> We should
> take a day off.

MRS. SAMSA.
> Yes, yes,
> we deserve one.

GRETE SAMSA.
> I think
> we certainly
> *need* one.

MR. SAMSA.
> Let's each
> sit down and write
> a letter of excuse to our
> supervisors.

MRS. SAMSA.
> We must
> absolutely
> do that.

GRETE SAMSA.
> I could
> simply not miss
> without
> some sort of an
> excuse.

(The **CLEANING WOMAN** *emerges from Gregor's room having wrapped Gregor's body in the rug which she has already taken out for trash. She pauses, dramatically, on her way to the front door.)*

MR. SAMSA.
> Yes? Yes?

MRS. SAMSA.
> What do you want?

CLEANING WOMAN.
>You won't
>have to worry
>about getting rid of ...
>that "stuff" next door. It has all been
>disposed
>of, well enough.

>*(**THE SAMSAS** resume their writing.)*

>Well...I ...

>*(**MR. SAMSA** raises his hand, stopping her. SHE turns
>abruptly, insulted.)*

>Good day
>to every one.

>*(Slams the front door)*

MR. SAMSA.
>We will
>fire her tonight.

>*(**GRETE** and **MRS. SAMSA** go over to the window
>and hold on to each other.)*

>Come on now, stop brooding over
>the past
>and please have some
>consideration for me too.

>*(The WOMEN come back and give him a hug.)*

We'll take
a trolley to
the open country outside the
city,
we will enjoy
the warm sunshine and talk
about our opportunities.

MRS. SAMSA.
We can,
perhaps move to
a smaller apartment,
and that would be an immense help.

MR. SAMSA.
And one
better suited
to our needs, easier
to manage than this, and not so
badly
located as
this one that our Gregor picked out.

MRS. SAMSA.
And look
at Grete now,
how pretty she is. Why
what rosy cheeks and how shapely
she has
become. It will
be time, soon, to find a
husband for her.

*(The **SAMSAS** get up to leave. At the door **GRETE** stretches her youthful body. The family departs and the **FIDDLER** rises, again playing his wild and poignant music, then he, too, exits.)*

ACT III SCENE 3

*(The **STAGE MANAGER** appears again on the stage alone, the clock ticks.)*

STAGE MANAGER.
Gregor awoke from disturbing dreams....

(The stage goes black)

THE END

*   *   *

INTERVIEW WITH E. THOMALEN BY NEW YORK THEATRE VOICES

newyorktheatre.com: nytheatre voices
Your play is called *Metamorphosis, From Kafka*. What exactly does that mean and how much real difference is there between your text and the original?
My adaptation is actually called *The Metamorphosis; A Play*. We called the show *The Metamorphosis from Kafka* in order to distinguish it from Mary Zimmerman's *Metamorphoses* which is actually from Ovid. They are, of course, quite different plays. Kafka's tale is very focused, very condensed and very early 20th century. Ovid's stories are drawn from classical mythology and involve several different legends with different lessons.

But aside from identifying the source, *The Metamorphosis from Kafka* actually captures a deeper truth about my interpretation of the novella. The recent Kafka exhibition at the Jewish Museum shows how much his work was autobiographical. This can also be seen in his *Diaries 1910 – 1923*. Many of the choices that I made in adapting the novella were made with this in mind. Franz Kafka was a wildly ambitious, deeply sensitive and passionate individual who despised his job filled with endless filing cabinets and numbing paperwork. He desperately wanted to be a successful writer. At a personal level, the Diaries tell us that he had trouble sleeping and experienced very vivid dreams. Also that he had trouble at times in awakening from his dreams. I have used the device of Gregor awakening into a dream, which gives us a window into the dreamer and is something that can be represented well on the stage. The Stage Manager in the play summons the audience to experience it as Gregor does. The story has certain common hallmarks of a nightmare, e.g. the inability of the dreamer to communicate with other figures in the nightmare and the

84

inability to affect the action in any way desirable to the dreamer. Dreams can be considered metaphors and, perhaps, one reason that a dreamer cannot alter them during sleep, is that it would alter the meaning the dreamer is trying to depict to himself. I have chosen to represent Gregor (Kafka) via the dual means of an actor who conveys Gregor's feelings through mime and a fiddler who conveys the internal feelings that consume him.

The family is represented conventionally and as Kafka saw them. One can see in the diaries that they are modeled after members of his own family. His feelings about his Father were elaborated in his famous long "Letter to his Father". His Father comes across very much as the competent worker and provider for his family but lacking in any awareness of his son's soul or support for his ambitions. Kafka put copies of his books on his Father's bedside table but his Father never read them. His Mother was more patient but similarly obtuse. For example, in an entry in December 1911 Kafka writes: "Today at breakfast I spoke with my Mother by chance about children and marriage, only a few words, but for the first time saw clearly how untrue and childish is the conception of me that my mother builds up for herself. She considers me a healthy young man who suffers a little from the notion that he is ill. The notion will disappear by itself with time; marriage, of course, and having children would put an end to it best of all. Then my interest in literature would also be reduced to the degree that is perhaps necessary for an educated man. A matter-of-fact, undisturbed interest in my profession or in the factory or in whatever may come to hand will appear. Hence there is not the slightest, not the trace of a reason for permanent despair about my future. There is occasion for temporary despair, which is not very deep..." Compare that to Mrs. Samsa in the play: "I think the best idea would be to try to keep the room as it was before, so that when Gregor comes back to us once again he will find things unchanged and can forget all the more easily what has happened in the meantime." Grete I think is more of an amalgam of sisters and perhaps other girls Kafka had known.

Why did you decide to do this play and what did you hope to accomplish by it?

Many readers who have read the play, have commented on the apparent absence of Gregor in the script because he has no spoken lines, as though, somehow, spoken lines only a play make. Of course that is absurd as anyone who has seen *Contact* can attest. A playwright should be judged not on how clever his dialogue is, but on what his writing makes possible on the stage. By having the character of Gregor represented by a mime accompanied by a musician who can capture the wild swings in his feelings, the part has been left open to the individual artist's imagination, the creativity of the Director and the Actor. Unleashing such talent is the gift of good playwriting and I do not find it surprising that all of the reviewers who have written about the show have loved the performance of Kevin Whittinghill even if they have been critical of my adaptation, etc.

The play is done in verse. Why did you choose this form and what do you think this adds to the piece?

The play is written in a peculiar verse form called a "Cinquain". A Cinquain is a five-line structure of increasing number of syllables returning in the fifth line to that of the first (2-4-6-8-2). I have modified that form since not all speeches can precisely fit that sequence and probably would be boring if they did. The advantage of using it is that it approximates, or is suggestive of, German and middle European speech patterns that I have heard. Recently I was listening to a Saturday matinee Metropolitan opera broadcast of a German opera and I could pick up a very similar cadence.

Could you tell us a bit about your background and education that sparked your interest in Kafka and enable you to write this?

I first became interested in adapting Kafka's novella after completing a play about the life of German artist Käthe Kollwitz. An important part of the Kollwitz play dealt with the Nazi holocaust. After World War I, Germany failed to metamorphose into a responsible democratic republic as people had hoped, instead transforming itself into a horrible and horrifying regime. Symbolically, a culture changed itself into a hideous bug. I wondered if Kafka had any answers. I have come to see that Kafka's story is really more personal than political or cultural however.

The play has just been extended, so the audiences have enjoyed it and spread the word. What have you heard from people who have seen the play and is this what you expected?
Personal comments from people one knows are, of course, uniformly very kind. But the reviews have been interesting and seem to vary by gender. Women reviewers have been very sympathetic and understanding of the piece. But male reviewers have been very critical to caustic, with a few exceptions. I think in some ways it threatens men and that has made me think more about why that is. My guess is that it touches on a very sensitive area of Father/son relationships which are perhaps more comfortably handled by Mothers and daughters. The novella and play are cautionary tales and one of the things that Kafka seems to be saying is: Father don't treat my differences as horrible and make me have to hide them or I shall end up unable to be myself, function, or even live. He wanted his Father to hear that message but his Father never read his books and Kafka was unable to give him his letter. Kafka, however, also was unable to recognize the cautionary message in the tale/dream for himself: that to survive he did need to say it to his Father.

Do you have plans to do this play in other venues?
At the moment there are no other plans or venues. I do feel that its message is important and such reflection is needed in our busy lives where so little time is permitted for this activity.

In your opinion what does *METAMORPHOSIS* say about our time and why do you feel it has become a classic?
Kafka suffered and struggled with being different and it is what I think attracts us to his writing. He knew what it meant to be an outsider in so many ways. We all experience that in one way or

another and he provides both the comfort of someone who has been there and understands as well as some cautionary words that are worth listening to.

MURDER AT THE GREY'S HOUND MANSION
Maxine Holmgren

Mystery, High School/ Community Theatre /5f, 3m/ Simple Set
This is a mysterious comedy (or a comical mystery) that will have everyone howling with laughter.

The eccentric owner of Grey's Hound Mansion has been murdered. The cast gathers at the gloomy mansion for the reading of the will. Lightning lights up the stage as thunder and barking dogs greet the wacky characters that arrive. Each one is a suspect, and each one suspects another. Mixed metaphors and alliterations will have the audience barking up the wrong tree until the mystery is solved.

Baker's Plays
7611 Sunset Blvd.
Los Angeles, CA 90046
Phone: 323-876-0579
Fax: 323-876-5482

BAKERSPLAYS.COM

A FATHER'S SECRET
Alexandra Dennett

Drama / 6m, 2f / Area staging

What if your entire world is taken away from you, twice? Paige was seven when her parents died in a car accident, and ever since then one of their friends, Eddie, has taken care of her. He's a strict guardian, but she has an active life and good friends and generally enjoys a rather stable and happy existence. Then one day, eight years after Eddie took her to live with him, the police barge in and arrest him for kidnapping her. They inform her that her parents weren't dead when he took her away, and that her father is still alive. But Eddie has been her sole parent, and a good one, for the majority of her young life and Paige resists the ever-growing realization that the man she trusts most is not who she thought he was.

Winner of the 2007 Baker's Plays High School Playwriting Competition

Baker's Plays
7611 Sunset Blvd.
Los Angeles, CA 90046
Phone: 323-876-0579
Fax: 323-876-5482

BAKERSPLAYS.COM

IN JULIET'S GARDEN
Judy Elliot McDonald

Comedy / 7f, (1m optional) / Simple staging
Juliet Capulet invites four other heroines of Shakespeare's classics (Katharina, Portia, Ophelia and Desdemona) to lunch in her favorite garden in Verona to discuss 'issues' they all have with their plots. All the ladies have suggestions how these issues might be remedied. Shakespeare has also been invited, but instead sends an envoy, his literary agent and editor Jacqueline de Boys, who attempts to save the day with the help of Juliet's Nurse. This lively fifty-minute one-act comedy sparkles with wit and an in-depth understanding of the characters of these indelible ladies, and their effects on playgoers over the centuries. (Cameo appearance by Shakespeare at the end is optional).

Baker's Plays
7611 Sunset Blvd.
Los Angeles, CA 90046
Phone: 323-876-0579
Fax: 323-876-5482

BAKERSPLAYS.COM